I Will Paint!

by Miriam Sklar

ISBN: 978-1-338-75078-2
Illustrated by John Lund

Published by Scholastic Inc., 557 Broadway, New York, NY 10012

10 9 8 7 6 5 4 68 25 26 27/0

Printed in Jiaxing, China. First printing, January 2021.

I will paint a tree.

I will paint a flower.

I will paint a bug.

I will paint a sun.

I will paint a cloud.

I will paint a bird.

I will paint a rainbow!